a min dition book

published by Penguin Young Readers Group

Text copyright © 2007 by KNISTER

Illustrations copyright © 2007 by Mandy Schlundt

Original title: ...ja, wenn das so ist

English text translation by Kathryn Bishop

Coproduction with Michael Neugebauer Publishing Ltd., Hong Kong.

Rights arranged with "minedition" Rights and Licensing AG, Zurich, Switzerland.

Published simultaneously in Canada.

Manufactured in China.

Typesetting in Nueva by Carrol Twombly.

Color separation by Mandy Schlundt.

Library of Congress Cataloging-in-Publication Data available upon request.

ISBN 978-0-698-40056-6

10 9 8 7 6 5 4 3 2 1

For more information please visit our website: www.minedition.com

KNISTER

Sophie's Dance

With Pictures by
Mandy Schlundt

Translated by Kathryn Bishop

minedition

Whenever Sophie's mother and father go out, Sophie gets to sleep
over at Grandma Elizabeth's house. That was the way it was this
weekend. Her parents dropped her off, and Grandma asked them,
"Are you going to the big dance tonight?"
"No, we're going to a birthday party at the home of some friends,"
said Sophie's mother.
"Oh," said Grandma. "Well, have fun!"
Sophie waved goodbye to her parents.
"What kind of dance is it?" asked Sophie.
"It's a big dance that only happens once a year," explained Grandma.
"When your grandfather was alive we always went to the dance.
We had such fun. We danced every dance."

"Why don't we go to the dance?" Sophie suggested.
"No, the dance is late. Children belong in bed at that time of night," explained Grandma Elizabeth.

"But I want to go to the dance," said Sophie.
"Sophie," said Grandma, "a dance like that starts when it is nearly dark and lasts till late at night. Children are too young for such celebrations, and grandmas are too old."
"No, no, no," said Sophie. "Celebrations like that are very good for children — they can learn a lot, especially from their grandmas."
"Oh, they can, can they?" asked Grandma.

"Yes, they can, and the grandmas can also have a lot of fun — especially if their grandchildren are there," said Sophie.

"Well, if that's the way it is…" Grandma laughed, "Then we'd better get going."

"Let's hurry up," said Sophie. She was starting to get excited.

"First, I have to get ready, I want to look pretty," said Grandma.

"But you are already pretty," said Sophie.

"For something this special you have to be especially pretty," said Grandma.

"Now you are pretty enough,"
said Sophie. "Let's go!"
"No, no! For a dance one has to
look extra, extra pretty,"
said Grandma.

"But now you're ready, aren't you?"
asked Sophie.

"Not quite," said Grandma.

"One more important thing –"

"My party dress!
Your grandfather always liked
this dress. What do you think?"
asked Gramda. She was a little
unsure.
"You look beautiful," said Sophie.
Grandma Elizabeth smiled.
"A long time ago," she said, "when
your grandfather was still alive,
he used to say, 'Elizabeth, you are
so beautiful, you're as beautiful
as summer.' He liked to make me
happy."

Sophie went to the mirror and asked.
"What about me? Am I pretty enough
to go to the dance?"

"You always look lovely and, at your age
beauty doesn't need any help," said Grandma.

"Well, if that's the way it is…." smiled Sophie.
"Besides, I've grown and my favorite dress
doesn't fit any more. I'm just too big."

Grandma Elizabeth laughed,
"That's a problem I have with some of my dresses."
Then they were off.

The dance was wonderful, even better than Sophie had imagined.
Everyone was laughing and joking, and they all looked very happy.

A band was playing, and people were dancing in the glow of multi-colored lanterns. Sophie wasn't the only child. She saw three other children, and even their dog was dancing.

"I'll be right back," Sophie said and ran to play with the other children.

When Sophie came back Grandma Elizabeth wasn't at their table. Sophie looked all around.

Where was she?

Was she having
something to drink?

Maybe she went to
get her sweater.

Was she in the restroom?

Could she be on the dance floor?

Finally she saw her grandmother,
but she wasn't alone. Sophie ran to her.

"Well, here you are," said Grandma.
"Sophie, I'd like you to meet Mr. Bunting.
He is such a marvelous dancer. I feel as
light as a feather."

"How much longer will you be dancing?"
asked Sophie. Sophie would rather have
had her grandmother all to herself.

"Why don't you dance with us?" asked
Mr. Bunting.

"Oh, I don't know," said Sophie. "How long
will you keep dancing?"

"I don't know..." said Grandma.

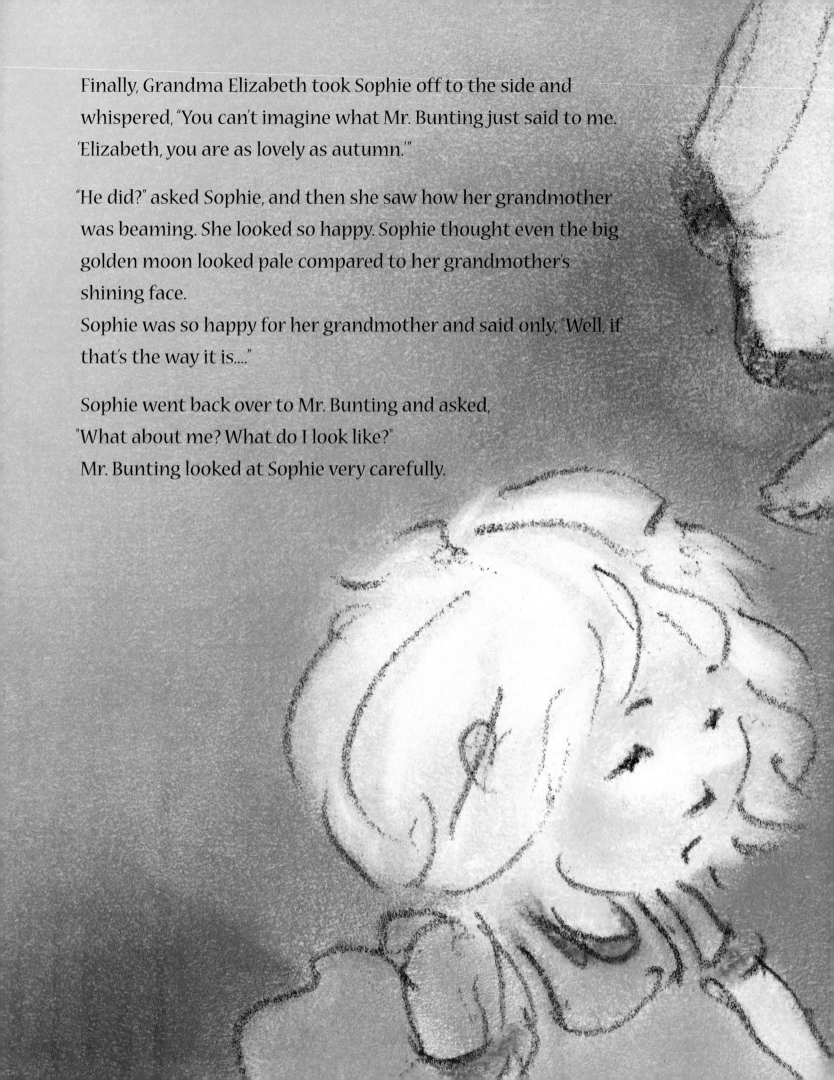

Finally, Grandma Elizabeth took Sophie off to the side and whispered, "You can't imagine what Mr. Bunting just said to me. 'Elizabeth, you are as lovely as autumn.'"

"He did?" asked Sophie, and then she saw how her grandmother was beaming. She looked so happy. Sophie thought even the big golden moon looked pale compared to her grandmother's shining face.

Sophie was so happy for her grandmother and said only, "Well, if that's the way it is...."

Sophie went back over to Mr. Bunting and asked,
"What about me? What do I look like?"
Mr. Bunting looked at Sophie very carefully.

Finally he said,
"Sophie, you are as pretty as springtime."

Sophie couldn't tell if it was Mr. Bunting or
Grandma Elizabeth, or
if it was this wonderful evening
that made her feel lighter
and lighter...
and lighter...

"You know," said Sophie. "I'm so happy, I think I could fly!"
Grandma laughed and said,
"Well if that's the way it is...."

And so with the moon looking on,
they flew lighter and lighter,
dancing until they almost touched the stars.

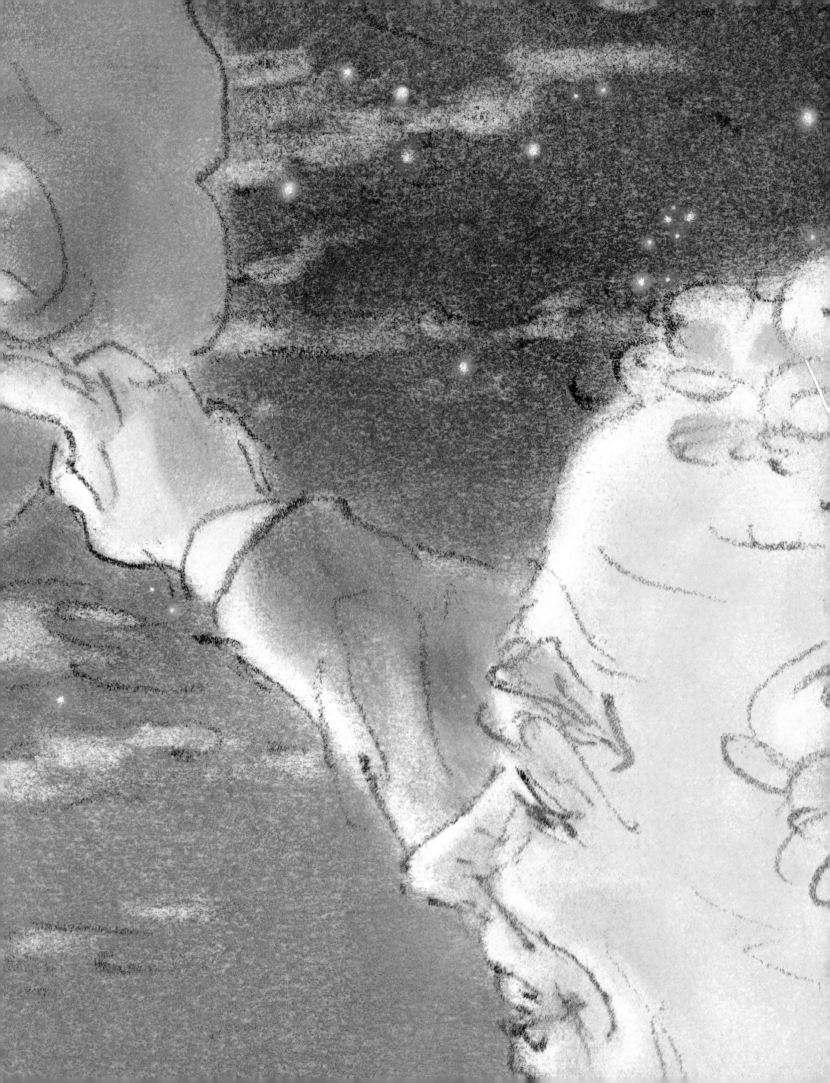